H

Heroes

Time to Speak Up

Written By

Glen Mourning

ISBN: 979-8-7298288-4-5

DEDICATION

In a world full of challenges, children may have it the hardest when it comes to learning how to make the most out of life. And when you are fortunate enough to make it to adulthood, remember that along the way, some grown-ups cared deeply for you. This book is dedicated to kids and hardworking adults who want to make the world a better place.

ACKNOWLEDGMENTS

To my mother, Lillian
Without your support and unconditional love, I would have indeed given up on myself as a young man and as a student. Attending school was challenging, but when I learned how education could open the door to a better tomorrow, I learned to wake up each morning with a purpose. You made me believe in me! Thank you to all of the fantastic parents, guardians, teachers, coaches, and mentors around the world. Your efforts are necessary and appreciated.

Never give up.
Success is on the other side of your struggle.

Reading Standard question stems for developing strong independent thinkers

Why did (event) happen? How do you know? • What does (character) think about (event)? How do you know? • What do you think (character) will do differently next time? • Explain why (character or object) is important to the story.

What happened at the beginning, middle, and end of the story? • What is a summary of this story? • What is the lesson you should learn from this story? • What is this story trying to teach?

How does (character) feel at this part of the story? How do you know? • How does (character) actions change what happens in the story? • What problem does (character) have in

the story? How does he/she solve their problem?
• How does (character) change throughout the story? • What are (character) personality traits? How does his/ her personality affect what happens in the story? • Why is the setting important to the story?

How are the parts of the story connected? How does this section/chapter help the reader understand the setting? • How does this scene build suspense? • How would you retell this story, including important parts from the beginning, middle, and end? • Why did the author organize the story like this? How would it be different if the order were changed?

Who is telling this story? How do you know?
• From what point of view is this written? •

Time to travel back and save history!

Contents

Chapter 1: Big Shoes to Fill

A long time ago a group of kids walked along a dirt road. "Man, I sure wish I had some ice-cold water," one of the boys said. They lived in the South where it was very hot. The kids were only eight-years old but had to hike to school on their own. They argued about if their friend had enough courage to grow up to become like his father. "I can do it!" the boy shouted.

"Yeah, right! You get nervous just thinking about," the oldest boy replied.

When the kids got to class their friend was given a chance to prove his bravery.

"It's your turn Martin," Mrs. Brown called out. "Please make your way to the front of the room. We don't have all day."

Mrs. Brown was their 3rd grade teacher. She was kind and loving but was running out of patience with Martin. "Come on, don't be shy Martin. You're the last one," Mrs. Brown said encouragingly.

It was time for Martin to show the boys that they were wrong. "I can be like my father," Martin said to himself. But even though he loved school, being asked to read out loud was a nightmare.

In America during those times, all the Black students went to one school and all the White students went to another. Martin did not like the way life was. He could play with his White friends at home, but he was not allowed to go to school with them. Martin knew that the way things were for Black and White people was wrong. So, he chose to write about it. But he was too shy and nervous to read his writing in front of his classmates. Mrs. Brown gave Martin one last chance. But then Martin heard the boys in class laugh at him.

"Told you that you won't ever be like your dad," his classmate shouted.

Martin crumpled up his writing and put his head down on the desk. Would he find the courage to read in class? Or would he let the fear in the back of his mind stop him forever?

Chapter 2: History Lovers

Those boys made fun of Martin a long, long time ago. But not all kids feel the way Martin did about school.

Kayla and Daniel Jones love being in 3rd grade. They live-in present-day Washington, D.C. and the two of them are brother and sister. It's hard to tell by just looking at them, but they are twins. Soon they will become the most important kids in the world.

"Let's go Kayla, we are going to be late for school," Daniel shouts. "You know history is my favorite subject."

"Hold your horses, I'm coming," Kayla says. "I love history too. And it's Friday. So, you know what that means?" The twins finally head off to school.

But each week, they realize that no one loves history as much as their teacher Mrs. Robinson does. On Fridays she teaches her class about an important person from the past. And then on Monday mornings, the class learns all about that person. Mrs. Robinson loves the challenge of teaching new things. Luckily, she doesn't have to convince Kayla and Daniel that school is fun. But soon, the twins will face a challenge of their own.

Chapter 3: Bad Timing

The twins have attended Elite Public Charter School since kindergarten. And even then, they were always one step behind. Luckily, there is a metro bus that takes them directly to school. "Man, that was close," Daniel says.

They get to school a few minutes late. Daniel eats his favorite snack for breakfast.

"Sorry Daniel. We'll leave the house earlier next time," Kayla says. She knows her brother hates missing class.

"It's okay. I can't wait for this lesson to start," Daniel whispers.

Kayla and Daniel are the most excited kids in the school. They are also two of the coolest kids in town. Well, not really.

"Daniel, you have flaming hot Cheetos all over your shirt," Kayla says.

Quietly, Daniel brushes the crumbs from his chest. Not only is he a messy eater, but the kids always pick him last to play at recess.

Daniel puts his backpack away and takes his seat. He takes out his notebook to prepare for class. "Man, I need new glasses. These things are always falling off my face," Daniel says with a sigh.

Daniel forgot his homework on the kitchen table back at the house. "Dang, I'll be missing out on shopping at the school store again," he complains.

Daniel is having a rough morning. He just hopes that today no one makes fun of him for how dark his skin is. Although many of the 3rd graders are African American, Daniel is a lot darker than most of them. Sometimes Kayla's caramel brown skin makes kids think that the two of them aren't even related.

Kayla hands in her homework and takes out her notebook. "Five more points for me," Kayla says.

"Good morning Kayla," Rodney says. "Hope you pick me today at recess." Kayla is always chosen as a team captain when the kids play sports.

Kayla smiles and is ready for class. Deep down inside, she believes that she knows the answer to everything. But sometimes her attitude gets her into trouble. Just then, Cody, one of the class clowns passes his best friend Miles a note and the two boys seem to be up to no good.

Chapter 4: The Big Sister

The lesson is about to start. Daniel walks back to his seat from sharpening his pencil. Miles sticks out his foot and Daniel hits the ground. "Look at the loser," Cody shouts.

"What's the matter, four-eyes? Can't see where you're going?" Miles asks sarcastically.

Although they are twins, Kayla takes on the role as the *big* sister. The class sees Kayla's eyes light up with anger. She walks right over to Miles and Cody. She balls up her fists and stomps her feet. "Bullies, just stupid bullies," she screams.

"Kayla!" Mrs. Robinson shouts. "Lower your voice and return to your seat immediately."

Mrs. Robinson moves Miles and Cody apart from one another. "And as for you two boys, don't ever think about messing around in my classroom again," Mrs. Robinson commands.

Chapter 5: Who is the King?

The class seems to be a bit rowdy, but they care quickly put in check. Mrs. Robinson isn't like other teachers who send kids to the principal's office. Instead, she deals with problems her own way. The class settles down. Then, a strong voice sweeps over the room.

"Darkness cannot drive out darkness, only light can do that. Hate cannot drive out hate, only love can do that," Mrs. Robinson says.

"Does anyone know where this quote is from?"

The students sit in silence for a moment. They all look around the room to see if anyone knows the answer. And then Mrs. Robinson shouts out again.

"I have a dream that my four little children will one day live in a nation where they will not be judged by the color of their skin but by the content of their character," Mrs. Robinson says pressing her hands over her heart.

The class is still silent.

"Come on, you all have to know that one," Mrs. Robinson shouts.

But no one seems to know what Mrs. Robinson is talking about.

"Those are quotes from Dr. Martin Luther King Jr. He led the Civil Rights

Movement. Without him and the help of his friends, people would still be divided by race. Life wouldn't be the same without his words," Mrs. Robinson explains.

The students sit in silence as Mrs. Robinson continues.

"You can't go through life picking on each other because of your differences. I think hearing about Dr. King will be perfect for next week," Mrs. Robinson suggests.

The rest of the school day flies by. Before they know it, it's time for the kids to pack their bags and head to the buses. Kayla grabs her notebook and heads for the hallway.

"Not so fast young lady, we need to talk," Mrs. Robinson commands. Kayla drops her shoulders and her book bag drops to the ground with a loud thump.

Chapter 6: Learn to Lead

Class is dismissed, but Kayla stays behind for a moment. Daniel waits outside of the room.

"I know you want to protect your brother, but you have to find a better way," Mrs. Robinson says. "Don't let people anger you. Learn to be peaceful."

Kayla rolls her eyes. "It wasn't my fault," Kayla says as she crosses her arms.

"You are better than that," Mrs. Robinson say. "You have to be a leader."

Kayla nods her head and slowly walks out of the door. She finds Daniel and the twins run to catch their bus. After a quiet ride uptown, they are dropped off at their stop. They get to their house and their grandma is home waiting for them.

"Hey y'all, how was school?" Grandma Jones asks.

"Hey grandma," Kayla says.

"School was okay," Daniel says with a sad face. "It would have been better if

Cody and Miles didn't pick on me."

"Oh, well that doesn't sound good," Grandma Jones says. "What are they doing to you?"

The twins shout, "being bullies!"

"Ahh, well…that's got to stop," Grandma Jones states. "What did your teacher do about it?"

"Well, she didn't really do anything," Daniel says.

"Yeah, she just talked to us about some man named Dr. Martin Luther King Jr. She told us that we need to be kind to each other even if we are different," Kayla says.

Grandma Jones smiles from ear to ear. The twins couldn't believe what they were about to hear from her.

Chapter 7: Rich History

"When I was young your grandpa and I worked with Dr. King," Grandma Jones says.

Grandma Jones and her husband marched and fought for the rights of African Americans.

"I was even one of the first Black

teachers in the United States to ever work at a school with White students," Grandma Jones mentions proudly. "Are Cody and Miles White students?"

"Yeah, they are…but I want to be friends with them," Daniel says.

"I see. Well, long ago it was dangerous to be friends with White kids. Back in my day, people didn't accept the idea of Black people and White people doing much of anything together," Grandma Jones says.

"So, you and grandpa helped bring people from different races together like Dr. King?" Kayla asks.

One thing that the twins didn't know about their Grandpa was that he was an important member of the community.

"During his college years at Howard University he fought to make the country a better place. That is also what Dr. King did," Grandma Jones Says.

"I think that's what Mrs. Robinson was trying to tell us today in class," Kayla says.

"It's important to know how things used to be. You kids don't know how good you have it," Grandma Jones says. "Your grandpa fought for justice as a freedom fighter. He marched in the southern states with a man named John Lewis to make sure that you all could live better lives."

But Grandpa Jones was believed to be much more than an activist. What else was there for Grandma Jones tell the twins?

Chapter 8: Special Delivery

As a young man their grandpa dreamed of becoming an inventor.

"Oh, how I loved that man," Grandma Jones says. "He had ideas that were out of this world."

Sadly, the amazing Grandpa Jones died before the twins were even born. After spending his life as a hero, he had a heart attack. When he died, he may have had secrets that even Grandma Jones didn't know about.

Kayla walks into the living room to hang with Daniel before their parents come home. The doorbell rings.

"I wonder who that can be?" Kayla asks.

Their parents never ring the doorbell. Kayla looks through the peep hole, but she doesn't see anyone. Then Daniel looks for himself. "No one's there," Daniel says grumbling.

"Ugh, I know," Kayla says. "Maybe

it's just—."

Then, the doorbell rings again. This time there are two dings in a row. The twins hurry to answer. Kayla pulls the door wide open but to her surprise, no one is there.

"Yo! That's weird," Daniel yells.

"I give up," Kayla replies. "Maybe it's broken."

Just as they walk away the doorbell rings for a third time.

Kayla races to open the door even faster than last time. She turns the knob to see who is on the other side. The door swings open and knocks Kayla to the ground. Her mom and dad both walk into the house together.

"Hey, honey," Kayla's mother shouts. "What in the world are you doing on the floor?"

"Mom! Why are you and daddy ringing the doorbell like that?" Kayla questions. Kayla and Daniel are so confused.

"You know we don't ring the doorbell," Mr. Jones says. He laughs at how out of breath his children are.

"What kind of silly games are you and my little Danny getting into tonight?" Mr. Jones asks as he smiles.

Kayla scratches her head. "This doesn't make sense," she says.

Kayla is sure that the doorbell rang. Mr. and Mrs. Jones take off their coats and shoes to settle in.

"Hey Kayla, sweetie…can you please vacuum the living room and have Daniel sweep the kitchen floor before dinner?" Mrs. Jones asks. "Oh, and before I forget, this weird package was on the doorstep for you and your brother."

Chapter 9: A Dream Lives On

Kayla squints her eyes. Who could have sent her and Daniel a package? She stands near the front door and Mrs. Jones begins to walk upstairs.

"Mom, wait," Kayla shouts. "Who gave this to us?" Kayla asks.

"I don't know, girl…just open it,"

Mrs. Jones shouts.

Kayla looks puzzled. "Hey Daniel, we got a package. Let's open it together," Kayla suggests.

Daniel is clumsily sweeping the kitchen floor. He always rushes to get his chores done so he can squeeze in a game of NBA 2K before dinner.

"Do I have to?" Daniel asks. "You know I just want to finish cleaning so I can get online and play my game."

Daniel thinks about it for a second, then walks over to his sister.

"Okay, fine. Let's open it," Daniel says.

Kayla checks out the small package and notices that there are items inside. She carefully feels around the tightly packed envelop. The bubble wrap keeps her from really having any idea. Kayla and Daniel look each other in the eyes. And then Kayla slowly tears open the package.

A bright shinny light comes from the

package. Inside of the envelop is a sparkling gold sheet. Kayla takes it out. She realizes that the sheet is a letter. She holds up the glittery gold paper and sees a message addressed to her and Daniel.

"Woah...," Daniel says. Then Kayla begins to read it.

Chapter 10:
Surprise of a Lifetime

"Dear Freedom Fighters,

I can only imagine how incredible you two must be by now. This is way more important than playing video game so don't worry about that. And learn to ignore those kids at school. Don't let anyone bring you down. But, enough of that. I have much to explain. Inside of this package are my time travel inventions that I created a long time ago when I studied at Howard. As crazy as this sounds, I need you both to save history by traveling back in time. Once you finish reading this letter, the timer for your journey will begin. When the timer on your devices hit 00:00, they will bring you back to the present date and time and your mission will be over. Never let the devices fall into the wrong hands. There are people who might want to use them to ruin our country. You must travel back in time to the year 1937 and go to Atlanta Georgia. There, you will meet a boy named Martin. Find out his problem and solve it before it's too late. I know you two won't let us down. P.S, you must never reveal who you are or share the secret of your time traveling abilities with anyone. Now read the rest of the directions on the back of the letter. Move quickly. You don't have much time. Go now and become history heroes.

Love, Grandpa!

Kayla and Daniel couldn't believe their eyes. Their grandpa died before they were even born. How was this possible? And if the letter and time machines are real, what will Kayla and Daniel do next?

The twins flip over the letter and read the rest of the directions. The smart watches light up and beep. The clocks on the devices begin to count down! Kayla and Daniel hide the letter and put the devices away so that no one sees what they have.

"We can't let anyone find out about this," Kayla says. We need more time to figure out if these things are real."

"We?" Daniel says. "You're the only one who thinks that any of this is real. It's probably just mom and dad playing tricks on us."

"Oh yeah, how do you explain the gold shiny letter then? No one can make these" Kayla says. "You don't want to let grandpa down, do you?"

Chapter 11: Clueless

The weekend flies by but Kayla didn't sleep one bit. She spent every second worrying about the timer on her device. She wore it on her right wrist and thought about if time traveling was really a possibility. She put it on her left wrist and thought that there was no way that it could be true. She went back and forth all night dreaming of the possibilities. Finally, she placed it on her dresser and went to sleep.

Monday morning comes and Kayla prepare for school. Her eyes are droopy, and she is still tired. She puts the golden letter in her pocket. Next, she grabs her smart watch and hands the other one to

Daniel. They make their way to school.

"I can't believe you're making me wear this thing," Daniel says.

The twins get to school just as Mrs. Robinson begins the history lesson.

"Good morning my wonderful scholars," Mrs. Robinson says in a warm and welcoming voice. "Today might just be my favorite day of the year."

The students are used to hearing their teacher say that. It seems like every Monday is Mrs. Robinson's favorite day of the year. That's because of how excited she gets about teaching history.

Mrs. Robinson stands near the white

board. She turns off the lights and all the students are silent. The only thing visible is the light coming from the projector.

"Well, this is strange," Mrs. Robinson says. "Last Friday, I spoke to you all about being kind to one another. But now I can't remember who we are supposed to learn about today."

Kayla looks down at her wrist to check the timer on her watch. It lights up and she sees that there are only ten hours left before it reaches zero. The students look around at each other and can't remember who or what they are supposed to learn about either. Kayla and Daniel make eye contact with one another.

"Oh, class. Does anyone remember who the historical figure of the week is supposed to be for today?" Mrs. Robinson asks.

"Umm, maybe it's some smart lady like Mae Jemison" Charlotte says.

"No, no…I'm pretty sure it's a man," Kenny suggests.

One of the smartest 3rd graders in class is also stumped. "I can't quiet remember either," James says.

Mrs. Robinson opens the link on the computer. "Maybe this will help," she says. Mrs. Robinson presses play on the video, but the screen is completely blank.

Chapter 12: Careless Mistake

"That's odd," Mrs. Robinson says. "I've never had this issue."

The kids sit in almost total darkness. Cody and Miles giggle in the back of the room. You can always count on those two knuckleheads to make things worse. Mrs. Robinson glances around the room.

"Quiet down, or else we won't be able to start the video," she whispers.

Kayla shakes her head and then raises her hand.

"Yes, Kayla…can you help us?" Mr. Robinson asks.

"I don't know why no one else remembers but today we are supposed to learn about Dr. Martin Luther King Jr.," Kayla says smiling.

All at once, everyone jerks their heads in Kayla's direction. The room is silent.

"Dr. who, King what?" Cody asks. Everyone is used to Cody's jokes. Kayla assumes that he is messing around again.

"You know… Dr. King…The man who said I have a dream?" Kayla asks.

Everyone sits silently trying to understand why Kayla would make up such nonsense.

"Eh…okay. Thank you," Mrs. Robinson says scratching her head.

Another moment goes by.

"Ah, I got it," Mrs. Robinson shouts. "Let me check where I book marked my history lesson."

Mrs. Robinson opens her history book to the page that she plans to use. But the page is also blank!

"Okay class. We will put learning about our historical figure on hold for now. We will figure it out tomorrow," Mrs. Robinson says.

Pretty soon it's time for recess. Kayla plays soccer like she always does. She scores the winning goal and the kids on her team celebrate.

"Hey Kayla, awesome game," Rodney says as they slap high five. Recess ends and everyone walks over to their teachers to lineup.

But when Kayla reached up to celebrate with Rodney, the golden letter slipped out of her pocket. She didn't notice. She heads back into the building and leaves her letter behind.

"Hey, Cody…look," Miles whispers. While walking in line, Miles sees the golden letter and picks it up.

Chapter 13: Problems Arise

The rest of the school day flies by. Once again, the twins are off to catch the metro bus to head home.

During the bus ride, they think about their strange day. First, Mrs. Robinson forgot who the history lesson was supposed to be about. Then, the video link didn't play. On top of that, the history textbook was completely blank!

"Why in the world didn't Mrs. Robinson remember who we were supposed to learn about?" Kayla asks.

"I have no idea," Daniel says. "And how did the whole class forget about Friday?"

The twins continued thinking. "And did you see how everyone looked at me like I was the crazy one," Kayla asks.

Daniel looks down at his watch. "Do you really think these things work?" he asks. "It says that we only have two hours left."

Kayla reaches in her pocket for the

letter to read the directions again. "The letter," she shouts. "It was in my pocket all day, but now it's gone," she cries.

"What do you mean it's gone?" Daniel asks as he begins to look for it on the bus floor.

"That's what I said, Daniel. Kayla shouts. "Our letter is missing."

As the bus drives through the streets of D.C. Something about the city is different. Everywhere you look there are two buildings for almost everything. Certain stores have separate lines for customers. Weird signs about the *color* white hang on windows of all the shops. And no one seems to be getting along on the sidewalks. There are White men shoving Black men and Black men are shouting at White men up and down the block. But Kayla and Daniel are too distracted to notice.

"Wait a minute," Daniel whispers. "The letter said that we have to go back and help out *Martin*. Maybe Martin is the young Dr. Martin Luther King Jr!"

"Are you saying you believe that the time machine is real?" Kayla asks.

"Maybe everything that happened this morning was because we haven't traveled back in time to help Martin with his problem?" Daniel guesses.

Kayla thinks back to all that she knows about Dr. King and about Civil Rights. She thinks about what he stood for and who he inspired.

"If we don't complete the mission, Martin the kid will never turn into Dr. Martin Luther King Jr. the leader," Kayla shouts. "Daniel, we have to go and save history!"

Chapter 14: Not So Fast

The bus comes to a stop at the light.

"Look, Daniel…It's really happening," Kayla shouts.

The twins look out the bus window and see Black people and White people fighting and shouting at each other. It's as if life has gone back to the days of segregation!

"If we don't time travel and help Martin, more bad things will happen," Daniel whispers.

As the metro bus carries along, it stops much further away from where Kayla and Daniel usually get off.

"Alright, last stop of the day for your *kind*," shouts the bus driver.

"Your kind?" Kayla questions. "Does he mean because we're Black?"

"Oh no," Daniel shout. He can't believe what is happening. They are used to being dropped off much closer to home. Daniel is afraid.

"Don't worry Daniel. I'll handle this," Kayla says.

Kayla makes her way to the front to speak to the driver.

"Excuse me, bus driver sir. This isn't our stop. We have three more blocks to go," Kayla calls out.

"Hey," the driver shouts. "Do I look like I care?" he asks. "Now you and your little pal need to hurry up and get off this bus."

Kayla looks back at her brother and is unsure about what to do next. Something tells Kayla that arguing with the driver won't end well.

"Okay, Daniel…Sometimes we'll come across rude people. But it doesn't mean that we have to be like them," Kayla says. "We have much bigger things to worry about."

The twins grab their backpacks and jump off the bus to head home. The twins realize that they are running out of time to save history.

With Grandma Jones resting and their parents at work, Kayla and Daniel are torn. They think about the changes to their city that they saw on the ride home. They think about how much worse things can get.

They look each other in the eyes. "It's now or never, brother," Kayla says standing in the family living room.

She looks down at her smart watch and begins to panic. "Here goes nothing," Kayla says.

She carefully types the year 1937 into her watch and helps Daniel add Atlanta Georgia into his device. They follow the directions that were on the back of the letter and hold hands. At the exact same time, they press on the time travel button. Then, everything goes black.

Chapter 15: Not A Dream

The twins zap into thin air and disappear from Earth. They are spinning around and around at high speeds. They fall deeper and deeper into an endless black hole. Their eyes are closed as they scream for their lives. To them it feels like a lifetime, but only a few seconds passed.

But just then, the time machines work

exactly how Grandpa Jones designed them. The twins reappear. They are still holding hands and are safely on the ground. Instead of standing in their Washington, D.C living room, they are now outside and across the street from a beautiful yellow and brown house in Atlanta. The calendar on Kayla's phone says 1937. The GPS on Daniel's device says 501 Auburn Ave NE. They are at the King family home!

"We are here…we are really here," Kayla screams. "I can't believe it. I thought we were going to die in that black tunnel."

Daniel drops to his knees. He is in shock from being zapped into the past.

"Thank you, Jesus," Daniel shouts.

Kayla remembers what she read on the letter and decides what to do next.

"Okay, Daniel...I know this is crazy, but we have a job to do," Kayla commands.

She gets Daniel back on his feet. The twins look at the King's home. At first, the house seems empty. But then, Kayla sees the front door open.

"Look, Daniel...that has to be them," she whispers.

The twins cross the street. They see the King family coming outside.

"Be sure to lock the door, Martin," a man says with a deep voice. "Oh, and you better not chicken out like you've done at school. Move along boy…don't leave your speech in the house again," the man says.

The man is Martin's dad, Reverend Martin Luther King Sr. A shy and quiet boy is the last person to come out of the house. It's Martin! After hearing the words from his father, Martin puts his head down.

"Don't worry, brother. You got this," Martin's brother says.

Today Martin will have to give a speech and it's clear that something is wrong. Kayla and Daniel have confusion written all over their faces. They can't believe that they are really looking at a young Martin. Then, Kayla realizes that they must have traveled back in time to a specific day of the week.

Kayla and Daniel walk over to the King's front yard.

The reverend sees them. "Good morning, you two. You kids better be heading down to church now ya heard?" Reverend King Sr. says. "My boy is going to finally speak to the congregation about what it means to love your neighbor and to live in peace."

Kayla plays along. "Uh, yeah," she says. "My brother and I are heading over to the church right now."

Reverend King Sr. freezes. He refuses to take another step.

Chapter 16:
Something's Missing

"Excuse me?" Reverend King Sr. asks.

Kayla is confused. She looks at Reverend King Sr., then at Daniel and then looks back at the reverend. She doesn't know what to say. Luckily, Martin waves to get her attention. He mouths out the words, "yes, *sir*" with his eyes nice and wide.

Just then, Kayla gets it. "Oh, uh…Yes, Sir," she replies.

"Alright, now that's much better," the reverend says cheerfully.

Then the King Family walks down the sidewalk to the church.

Kayla and Daniel look down the road. They see crowds of people gathering to enter Ebenezer Baptist Church. They walk in their direction.

"It's so hot, Kayla," Daniel complains. "I need some water before I pass out."

"I know, Daniel," Kayla says. "But we have to keep going."

Kayla looks at her watch and panics. Kayla is still unsure about how they are going to help Martin. The twins finally get in the long line at the church. They slowly make it to the entrance.

"I bet you he chickens out again," a boy in front of Kayla says.

As the members of the church take their seats, Reverend Martin Luther King Sr. leads everyone in prayer. The choir sings and everyone sings along. The time comes for young Martin to give his speech. His father gives him a warm introduction.

"Brothers and sister, today…my son Martin will speak to you for the first time. I am excited for him to share a few words with the church. Put your hands together for Martin Jr.," the reverend shouts.

After a moment of clapping, the church goes completely silent. Martin is nowhere to be found.

Chapter 17: Hide and Seek

Kayla and Daniel sat in the back of the church to avoid being seen. But at that moment, the twins knew that they had to find Martin and encourage him to deliver his speech. Time is running out and they can't find Martin anywhere.

"I think he ran around the corner," Kayla yells. "This is our chance."

After a few moments of searching, Daniel decides to check the bathroom. That is where he usually hides when kids at school make fun of him. Daniel opens the bathroom door. Martin is there trembling and standing against the wall. He is holding his speech to his chest. His shirt is soaked from all his tears.

"Hey, Martin," Daniel says. "Are you alright? My name is…well…I'm a kid too and I know what it's like to be nervous." Martin looks up and dries his tears.

"Hello," Martin says. "I'm not nervous, I just don't think the people will like what I have to say," Martin says.

Daniel has been in Martin's shoes

before. "One time in my teacher's class, I had to read a poem in front of everyone. At first, I thought that the kids would laugh," Daniel says. Martin sees that Daniel can relate.

"But then I thought about how silly it was to care what the kids in my class thought. So instead, I used some advice that my sister gave me," Daniel adds.

"Advice?" Martin says as he wipes more tears from his face.

"Yeah, my sister told me to just read the poem out loud and pretend she was the only one in the room," Daniel replies.

Martin takes a deep breath and steps

away from the wall. He continues to listen to Daniel.

"How about this," Daniel says. "Go back out there and don't worry about if anyone likes what you have to say. Read what you wrote and imagine that it's just me, you, and your family out there. I'm sure they will love to hear what you have to say."

Martin gives it some thought and realizes that Daniel is right. He agrees that his family would love to hear what he's been so afraid to share.

"Gee, thank you. I guess I can give speaking in front of people a try," Martin says. Martin walks out of the bathroom, with a smile on his face and his head high. The reverend notices his son walking back into the auditorium and smiles. The crowd begins to cheer.

"And now, my son...Martin Jr. will give his speech," the reverend shouts.

Kayla and Daniel grab hands and watch from the back of the church as a young Martin Luther King Jr. takes the podium. Their smart watches begin to vibrate and beep. Three seconds later, they zap right off the face of the earth for a second time as everything goes black.

Chapter 18:
Grandpa's Wildest Dreams

Kayla opens her eyes and takes a careful look around the room. Daniel is on his knees again. This time he is smiling from ear to ear.

"Daniel, Daniel," Kayla calls. "Hey, bro…we are back," she shouts.

Then, Grandma Jones comes into the living room. "Back from where?" she asks.

Kayla looks at Daniel. He saves his sister from almost spilling the beans about their secret time traveling adventure.

"Oh, back from the kitchen…we just wanted to get a snack before dinner," Daniel says.

Grandma Jones gives her grandchildren a smirk. The family has dinner and after that the twins go off to bed.

The next day comes and it's time for school again. Kayla and Daniel are still in shock about their smart watches.

"I'm never taking this thing off," Daniel says. "That was amazing."

"What happens if mom and dad find out?" Kayla says. The twins think of ways to keep their devices a secret.

Kayla and Daniel make their way to the metro stop. The bus pulls up to the normal stop along its route. And when the twins get to school, there's a ton of excitement in their 3rd grade classroom.

"Good morning everyone and happy Tuesday," Mrs. Robinson says. "Today is a special day. We will learn about the amazing Dr. Martin Luther King Jr. Now keep your voices down and enjoy the video."

"I can't believe it," Kayla whispers to Daniel.

"My advice really worked," Daniel replies. Their first journey back in time was amazing! The kids sit back and learn all about what Dr. Martin Luther King Jr. did for America.

But in the back of the room, Miles places the golden letter on his desk. "They have to be in here somewhere," he says. "I'll find out who the history saving time travelers are if it's the last thing I do."

ABOUT THE AUTHOR

Glen Mourning is an educator and author. Crunchy Life Kid's books are his most popular work that consist of a multi-part series written for children ages 8 and up. As the oldest of his mother's five children, Glen's books tie in life memories, a spin on traditional fairy tales as well as his imagination to create heartfelt and mesmerizing stories.

Glen was blessed with the opportunity to lead by example where he would become the first of two generations to not only graduate from high school, but to complete a master's degree in pursuit of his dream of becoming a teacher.

In 2005 Glen earned a full-athletic scholarship to attend the University of Connecticut where he would make the "All Big East Conference" academic honor roll for two years in a row. Glen would complete both an English degree as well as a Women's Studies degree before graduating from UCONN to go on to attend graduate school at the University of

Bridgeport. In 2010 Glen finished his master's degree in Elementary Ed. and was named the Student teacher of the year at the University of Bridgeport.

More About Glen

At the beginning of his teaching career, Glen worked alongside of the nationally renowned educational contributor Dr. Steve Perry, star of the CNN special "Black in America II" and the host of TV One's "Save our Sons".

As an elementary teacher at Capital Preparatory Magnet School in Hartford Connecticut, Glen managed to brilliantly inspire the lives of hundreds of students in his tenure as an educator and football coach.

For the past several years Glen has worked as a language arts teacher where his creativity and brilliant approaches to learning have captured national attention. Glen has been featured in Ebony Magazine, People's Magazine as well as other nationally recognized news and media outlets. Glen has also written for PBS Teachers as an educational contributor. Glen travels the country speaking to students and educators all in hopes of inspiring the next generation of leaders.

Glen's other books include "Care More Than Us: The Young People's Guide to Success" which is accompanied by the "Young People's Guide to Success Student Workbook". These tools are great for building habits for successful futures as well as strong social and emotional skills.

His greatest accomplishments are not those that have occurred on the playing fields across America but rather with his promise to his family that he has kept for the last seven years which was to become the motivation for his students that have come from similar circumstances.

More from the Author

Crunchy Life Book 1:
Recess Detention

In book 1 of the Crunchy Life Series, students are challenged to think about what challenges they face daily that may distract them from being the best that they can be. Students often face problems that can easily overwhelm them, but what may also be hard for a kid to communicate to adults. Keep track of how Crunchy attempts to make smart choices in a confusing and challenging world. When times are tough, be sure to find positive people to surround yourself with.

Crunchy Life Book 2: Naughty or Nice

In book 2 of the Crunchy Life Series, students are challenged to think about times where they have had to serve a consequence after making a poor choice. Students often struggle with feeling as if they are bad kids. But sometimes kids make "bad" choices. Keep track of how Crunchy responds to his challenges. Always make good choices to avoid being naughty.

Crunchy Life Book 3: Tough Cookies

In book 3 of the Crunchy Life Series, students are challenged to have an open mind and hear from multiple perspectives. Students often struggle with learning new information, especially if it goes against what adults tell them. Keep track of how Crunchy grows as a thinker, as well as how he builds his confidence. Always be willing to learn new things!

Crunchy Life Book 4: One Piece at a Time

In book 4 of the Crunchy Life Series, students are challenged to differentiate between huge life problems and smaller problems that can be handled with coping skills. Students often struggle with thinking that no one understands how they feel. The truth is adults want students to learn how to persevere. Keep track of how Crunchy pushes through tough situations. Always accept responsibility for your actions.

Crunchy Life Book 5: Every Point Counts

In book 5 of the Crunchy Life Series, students are challenged to give 100 percent to the things that they set out to accomplish. Students often feel as though they are trying their best, especially on the things that they care about. However, with a little self-reflecting, students can find ways to dig deeper to improve their lives even more.

Crunchy Life Book 6: The Dream Chaser

In book 6 of the Crunchy Life Series, students are challenged to never let setbacks stop them from moving forward. Students often feel that events in life that have the power to cripple us mentally are worth holding on to and grieving over permanently. But sometimes, those devastating scenarios can be the single most encouraging event that promotes growth, resilience, and success. By reading some examples of triumphs, students can continue chasing their dream even after extreme situations.

Stay tuned for more adventures of History Heroes. Additional stories include time traveling to visit and save Jackie Robinson, Mae Jemison, Barack Obama, Beyonce, Muhamad Ali, Katherine Johnson, Marian Anderson and many more.

To submit your questions about Crunchy Life or to learn how to deal with challenging situations, email the Crunchy Life Education team at Booking@glenmourningcares.com

For more information, visit www.glenmourningcares.com

Made in the USA
Middletown, DE
02 March 2024

50120094R00061